The Burglar Next Door

By Alan Trussell-Cullen
Illustrated by Stephen Axelson

Chapter 1

The Flashing Light in the Night

Something woke Jenny in the middle of the night. She sat up in bed and turned on her torch. Perhaps a branch had tapped against her window?

She climbed out of bed and made her way
across the room to the window
to see if it was shut.
Outside in the dark
she could see the old house next door.
No one had lived in it for years
and now the garden was all overgrown.
It looked spooky in the dark.

Her brother Tim liked to tease her about it.
He said the old house was haunted
and that was why no one wanted to live there.

When he said things like this, Mum would say,
"Stop trying to scare your sister!
There's no such thing as a haunted house."

Jenny looked across at the old house now.
She shone her torch through the window
so she could see it better.
Then something very strange happened.
Someone flashed a light back at her!

"Oh no!" said Jenny.
"There's someone with a light
in the upstairs room!"

Chapter 2

Call the Police!

Jenny ran to her brother's room and shook him.

"Tim," she whispered.
"Wake up!"

Tim sat up in bed and rubbed his eyes.

"What's going on?" he asked.

"There's someone in the old house next door!" said Jenny.

"But no one has lived in that house for years," said Tim.

"Come and see for yourself, then," said Jenny.

TIM
ONLY

Tim followed Jenny to her bedroom.

"I just shone my torch like this," said Jenny.

Once again there was a flash of light
from the upstairs bedroom.

"You're right," whispered Tim.
"There's someone in that bedroom!"

"Every time I flash my torch,
they flash back," said Jenny.
"It's as if they are trying to send us a message."

"Someone could be holding them prisoner!"
said Tim.
"We had better get Dad and Mum."

They ran into their parents' bedroom and turned on the light.

"Dad!" shouted Tim.

"Mum!" shouted Jenny.

Dad jumped out of bed and Mum hid under the pillows.

"There's someone in the old house next door," said Tim.

"They keep flashing a light at us," said Jenny.

"It might be a burglar," said Dad.

"Or someone being held prisoner," said Tim.

"Call the police!" said Mum.

Chapter 3

Finding the Burglar

Dad telephoned the police and five minutes later a police car pulled up outside the old house. They all stood on the front step to watch.

The police banged on the door and called out, "Is there anyone in there?"

They didn't hear anything, so they gave the front door a push. To everyone's surprise, it opened.

"The door wasn't locked," said Dad.

"That's strange," said Tim.

"Very strange," said Jenny.

The police ran inside and up the stairs.

A few minutes later,
a policeman came out the front door again.

"Come over and meet your burglar
with the flashing light!" he called out to them.

"Is it safe?" said Mum.

"Very safe," said the policeman, with a big smile.

They all went into the old house.
Jenny shone her torch up the stairs.
It looked spooky in the dark.

"Come on up," said the policeman.

When they got to the upstairs room,
the policeman pushed the door open.

"Here's your burglar," he said.

Jenny looked into the room.

"I don't see anyone," she said.

"Over there," said the policeman.

Jenny shone her torch round to where he was pointing.

"It's a mirror," said Jenny.

"Yes," said the policeman. "The light you saw was your own torch light shining back at you!"

"Oh no!" said Jenny. "I guess that makes me the burglar!"

Everyone laughed.